"Youth is a quality,
not a matter of circumstances."
Frank Lloyd Wright

For Charlotte

Produced by the Department of Publications
The Museum of Modern Art, New York

Edited by Chul R. Kim with the generous participation of
Barry Bergdoll, Sara Bodinson, Emily Hall, Libby Hruska, Elizabeth Margulies,
Françoise Mouly, Peter Reed, Amanda Washburn, and Wendy Woon.

Designed by Frank Viva
Production by Frank Viva and Chul R. Kim
Printed in Korea by Taeshin Inpack Co. Ltd.
This book is typeset in MoMA Gothic and Franklin Gothic. The Paper is 150 gsm woodfree.

First edition 2013
© 2013 Frank Viva
Library of Congress Control Number: 2013935903
ISBN: 978-0-87070-893-0

Published by The Museum of Modern Art
Christopher Hudson, Publisher
Chul R. Kim, Associate Publisher

11 West 53 Street
New York, NY 10019-5497
www.MoMA.org

Distributed by Abrams Books for Young Readers, an imprint of ABRAMS, New York
Cover illustration by Frank Viva
Printed in Korea

YOUNG
FRANK
ARCHITECT
By FRANK VIVA

The Museum of Modern Art, New York

Young Frank's apartment is on the top floor of this tall building.

He is an architect.

He lives with his spotted dog, Eddie, and his grandpa, Old Frank, who is also an architect.

Young Frank makes things.

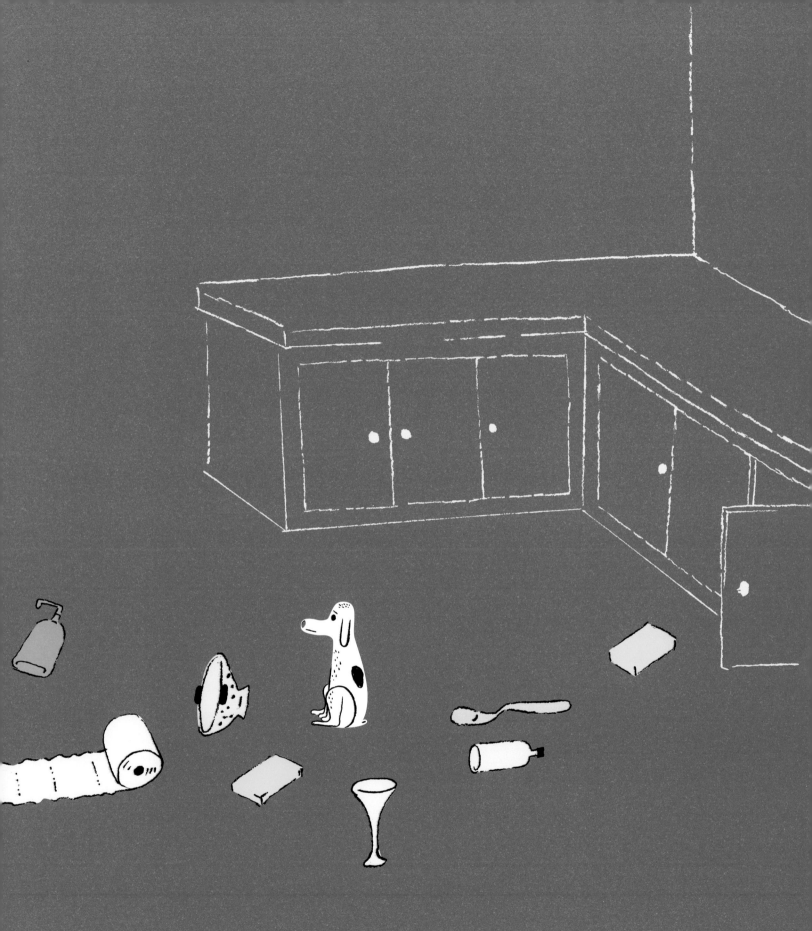

He uses anything he can get his hands on:
macaroni, books, dishes, spoons, dogs . . . Dogs?
Not Eddie! Yes, even Eddie. But only sometimes.

One morning, Young Frank made
a chair using toilet paper rolls.

"Hmm," said Old Frank, "I don't think architects make chairs. And you can't really sit in this one, can you?"

"I guess not," said Young Frank.

He also made a skyscraper out of books.

"Hmm, buildings should be straight," said Old Frank,
"not twisted and wiggly. Hey, are those MY books?"

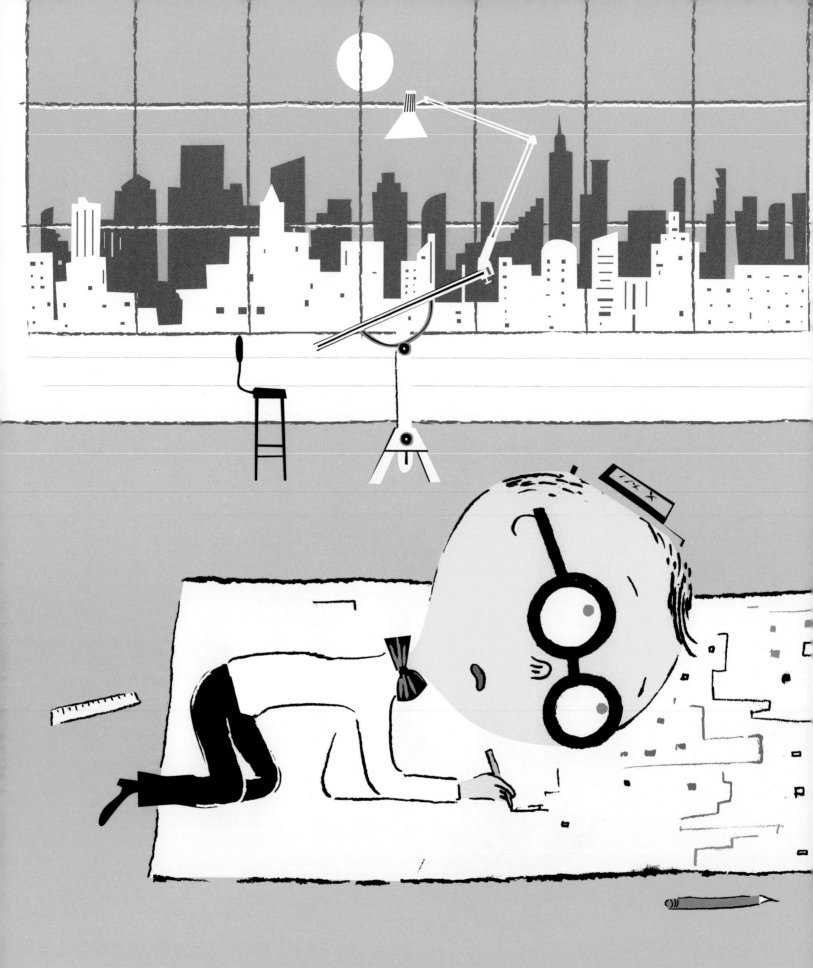

Just before lunch, Young Frank designed a whole city.

"Hmm," said Old Frank, "cities are made one building at a time and take hundreds of years."

At lunch, Young Frank said, "Grandpa, I'm not sure I want to be an architect anymore."

"Hmm," said Old Frank. "I know, let's go to the museum. I think it will be very good for you to see the work of some REAL architects. Don't you? Hmm?"

"I haven't been to the museum in years and years," said Old Frank.

"Me neither," said Young Frank.

They saw lots of things, including . . .

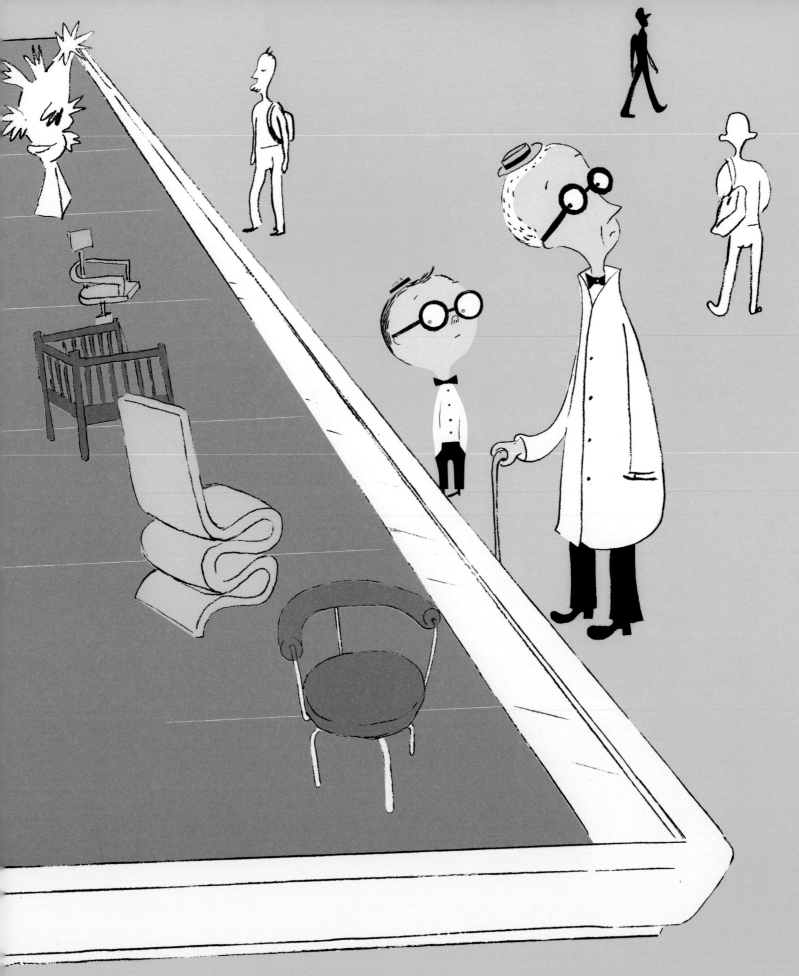

A wiggly chair designed by
an architect named Frank.

Old Frank looked
at it sideways.

A twisted tower by an
architect named Frank.

Old Frank cleaned
his glasses.

They also saw a giant model of a whole city
designed by another architect named Frank.

"Are all architects named Frank?" asked Young Frank.

"I don't think so," said Old Frank.

When they got home, Old Frank said, "Hmm, architects really do make chairs and twisted towers and cities, too. I guess I was wrong."

"That's okay, Grandpa," said Young Frank.
"Even I don't know SOME things."

That evening, Young Frank and Old Frank made chairs.
Chairs with zigzags. Chairs with crazy legs.

And a little chair that was perfect for Eddie.

They made buildings of every shape and size.
Tall ones, fat ones, round ones, and one made
from chocolate chip cookies.

"Eddie! Don't eat the library," said Young Frank.
"And please get back on your chair."

When they were done,
they had a whole city.

"Woof,"
said Eddie.

"Shh, Eddie," said Young Frank.
"Stay until I tell you. Good boy!"

Later that night, when Young Frank was tucked in his bed, he felt a bit older—like a REAL architect.

For his part, Old Frank felt younger—
and a little wiser.

"Woof,"
said Eddie.

The Museum of Modern Art in New York is a great place to bring children, both young and old. There are over 150,000 objects in the Museum's collection, and on any given day you might see two giant cheeseburgers by Claes Oldenburg, a guitar made by Pablo Picasso, and lots of other amazing modern and contemporary art. Here is a bit about the things that Young Frank and Old Frank saw—and the people who made them.

Frank O. Gehry

Frank O. Gehry is a Canadian-American architect, designer, and teacher. He has built lots of famous buildings, such as the Guggenheim Museum Bilbao in Spain and the Walt Disney Concert Hall in Los Angeles, which are known for their beautiful, twisty shapes. He also designed the Easy Edges Side Chair and the Hannover Tower, seen by Young Frank and Old Frank. When he was a child, Gehry and his grandmother used to build little cities out of scraps of wood.

Frank Lloyd Wright

Frank Lloyd Wright was an American architect and designer who thought that a building could be a "great living creative spirit" that nourished its occupants. Wright's Broadacre City model, which Young Frank and Old Frank see at the Museum, was his vision for a community. Eddie is named after a dog that Wright designed a house for in 1956 after receiving a letter from the pet's young owner. MoMA and Columbia University's Avery Library hold the Frank Lloyd Wright Archives.

Charlotte Perriand

 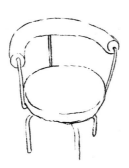

Charlotte Perriand was a French architect and designer known for working with new materials and technology. She was a founding member of France's Union of Modern Artists, a group of architects and designers. Young Frank and Old Frank see her Revolving Armchair, which she designed with Le Corbusier and Pierre Jeanneret, next to Gehry's Easy Edges Side Chair at the Museum.

Arthur Young

Arthur Young was an American inventor and helicopter expert who was also an artist, poet, astrologer, and philosopher. His dragonfly-like Bell-47D1 Helicopter, which hangs in MoMA's main lobby, was the world's first commercial helicopter. It was added to MoMA's Architecture & Design collection in 1984.

Visit www.MoMA.org to find out more about The Museum of Modern Art as well as these and other wonderful artists, architects, and designers.